SAMMY SPIDER'S
FIRST
TU B'SHEVAT

D0470372

KAR-BEN
PUBLISHING

A BOOK OF

To my children, Gabrielle, Shannan, and Jordan, responsible and caring adults who make me proud to be their mother.
—S.A.R.

Library of Congress Cataloging-in-Publication Data

Rouss, Sylvia A.
 Sammy Spider's First Tu B'Shevat / Sylvia Rouss; illustrated by Katherine Janus Kahn
  p. cm.
 Summary: Sammy Spider participates in the holiday of Tu B'Shevat by spinning a special web for his friend the tree.
 ISBN: 978–1–58013–065–3 (pbk. : alk. paper) [1. Spiders—Fiction. 2. Trees—Fiction. 3. Tu B'Shevat—Fiction.] I. Kahn, Katherine, ill. II. Title. PZ7.R7622 Sat 2000 [E]—dc21
                          00-044371

Published by KAR-BEN PUBLISHING, a division of Lerner Publishing Group, Inc. 1-800-4KARBEN www.KARBEN.COM

PJ Library Edition ISBN 978-1-5415-9861-4

Manufactured in China
1-48011-48730-6/17/2019

012033.8K1/B1467/A4

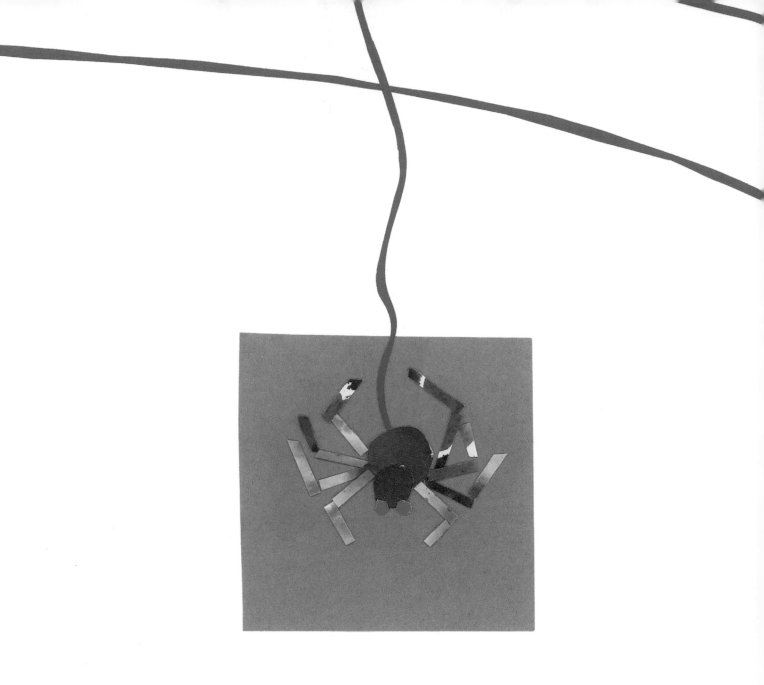

Sammy Spider was learning a new way to weave a web when he heard a scraping sound coming from outside the Shapiros' kitchen window.

"Look, Mother," said Sammy. "What are Josh and Mr. Shapiro doing?"

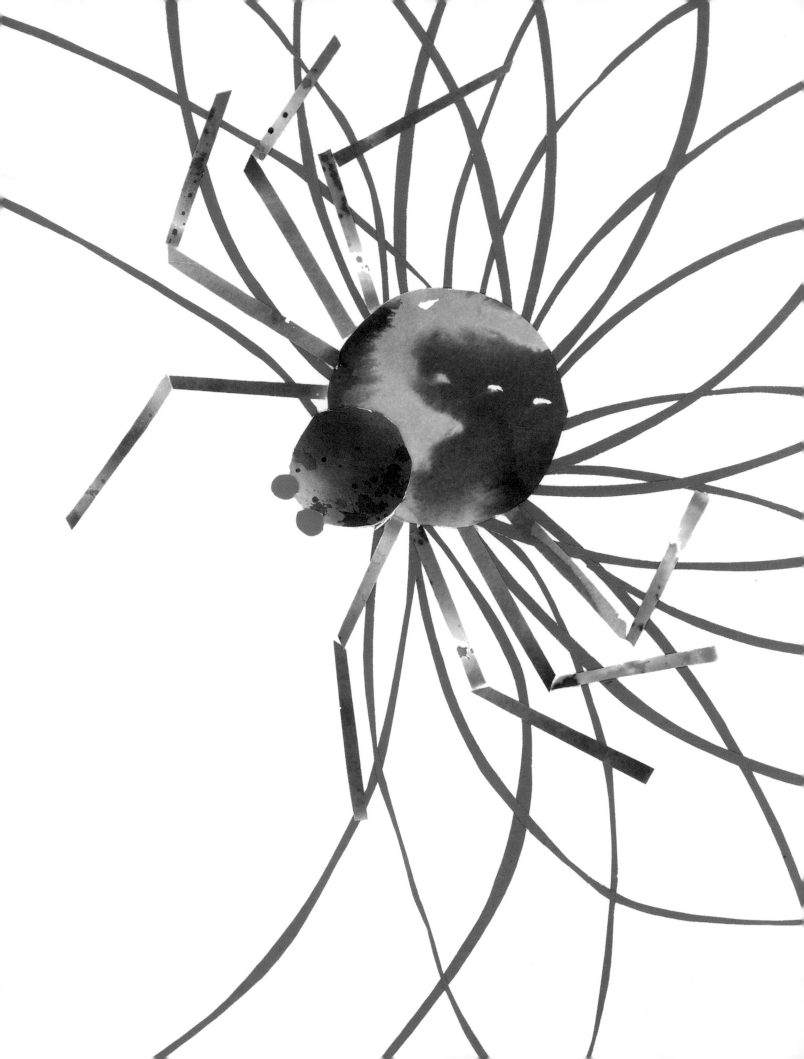

"It's early spring and they are planting," answered Mrs. Spider. Sammy watched as Josh and his father lowered the roots of a small tree into the hole they had dug.

"Will we plant a tree, too?" asked Sammy.

"Silly little Sammy," said Mrs. Spider. "Spiders don't plant trees. Spiders spin webs. Now watch me weave this pretty design into our web."

But Sammy wasn't listening. He was watching Josh water the tree with the garden hose.

"Trees need water to grow and lots of sunshine, too," replied Mrs. Spider.

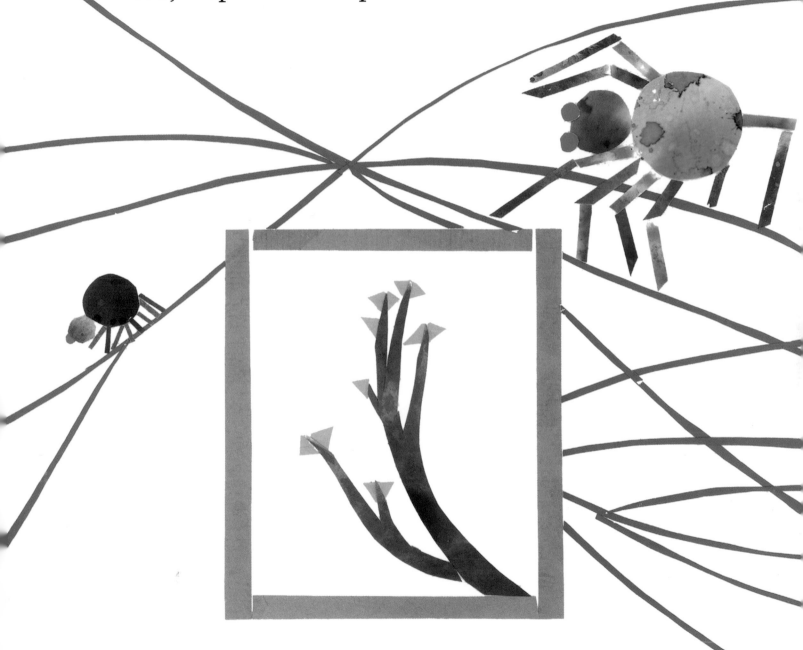

"Soon those little buds on the tree will blossom."

A few weeks later when Sammy peeked outside, he noticed buzzing bees and fluttering butterflies dancing among the blossoming buds. "Mother!" he shouted. "What are they doing?"

"They are drinking nectar from the blossoms," she said.

"Can I drink nectar too?" asked Sammy.

"No," laughed Mrs. Spider. "Spiders don't drink nectar. Spiders spin webs."

As the days grew warmer, Sammy noticed fewer blossoms. Finally, there were none. "What happened to the blossoms, Mother?" asked Sammy.

"It's summer now," said Mrs. Spider. "The blossoms have been replaced by bright green leaves."

Just then a bird swooped through the leaves and sat on a branch. She held a twig in her beak. Sammy watched her fly off and return with more twigs.

"What is the bird doing?" he asked his mother.
"She is building a nest, Sammy.

"Soon she will lay eggs,
and in a few weeks

little birds will hatch
from the eggs."

"Can we build a nest, too?" asked Sammy.

"Silly little Sammy," answered his mother. "Spiders don't build nests. Spiders spin webs."

Sammy woke each morning to the singing of the bird. He watched the eggs hatch and saw her feed her hungry babies. The baby birds grew and grew and one day when Sammy got up the nest was empty.

"Mother, what happened to the birds?" asked Sammy.

Mrs. Spider pointed to the tree. "See how the green leaves have turned red and yellow? Fall is here, and the birds have flown south where it is warmer. Now help me weave this pretty pattern into our web."

Sammy wasn't listening. He heard a scratching sound coming from outside and saw a little squirrel climbing up the trunk of the tree.

"Mother, what is the squirrel doing?"

"He's gathering food for the coming winter," she replied.

Each day Sammy watched the busy squirrel. The leaves began to fall off the trees until one day there were no more leaves. The squirrel no longer came to climb the tree. "It's winter and the squirrel is snug in his home," Mrs. Spider told Sammy.

Sammy shivered. "Mother," he whispered softly. "My friends are all gone. The bees, the birds, the butterflies, and now the squirrel."

"Not all your friends. The little tree is still here to greet you each morning," Mrs. Spider reminded him gently. "And look, I wove you a new blanket to keep you warm."

Sammy wished he could share his blanket with the little tree. During the winter months its bare branches were often covered with snow, and when the wind blew it seemed to tremble.

One crisp winter morning, Sammy awoke to a delicious smell. Mrs. Shapiro placed a freshly baked date nut bread on the counter next to a basket of nuts and dried fruit. "What's happening?" asked Sammy, looking down from his web.

"The Shapiros are celebrating Tu B'Shevat, the birthday of the trees. They will eat foods that grow on trees, and Josh will plant a sapling to celebrate the holiday," explained Mrs. Spider.

"Will we celebrate, too?" asked Sammy as Mr. Shapiro entered the kitchen.

"Silly little Sammy. Spiders don't celebrate Tu B'Shevat," said his mother. "Spiders spin webs."

Sammy came down off his web. He hopped onto Mr. Shapiro's cap just as he went outside to shovel snow away from the base of the little tree. While Mr. Shapiro worked, Sammy climbed onto the tree and began crawling in and out through its branches. When Mr. Shapiro finished, Sammy jumped back onto his cap, and they headed back inside.

"Where have you been?" asked a worried Mrs. Spider.

"I wove a birthday blanket to keep my friend warm," Sammy announced proudly.

Mrs. Spider saw the beautiful web shimmering in the branches of the little tree. "It's lovely!" she exclaimed.

"Happy Tu B'Shevat, little tree!" shouted Sammy. And as the wind came up, a branch with a tiny little bud seemed to wave back at him.